For Gina Shaw
— S.M.

Library of Congress Cataloging-in-Publication Data

Metzger, Steve.
It's apple-picking day! / by Steve Metzger; illustrated by Hans Wilhelm.
    p.   cm. — (Dinofours)
"Cartwheel books."
Summary: When Mrs. Dee takes the class on a trip to the apple orchard and Albert walks away from the rest of the group, Mrs. Dee explains the importance of safety rules.
    ISBN 0-590-03549-5
[1. School field trips — Fiction.   2. Safety — Fiction.   3. Nursery schools — Fiction.   4. Schools — Fiction.
5. Dinosaurs — Fiction.]
I. Wilhelm, Hans, 1945-   ill.   II. Title.   III. Series: Metzger, Steve. Dinofours.
PZ7.M56775Ip   1998
[E]—dc21   97-50574
                                                                                                          CIP
                                                                                                          AC

10 9 8 7 6 5 4 3   8 9/9 0/0 01 02

Printed in the U.S.A.   24
First printing, September 1998

DINOFOURS ™
IT'S APPLE-PICKING DAY!

by Steve Metzger
Illustrated by Hans Wilhelm

Cartwheel
·B·O·O·K·S·®

SCHOLASTIC INC.
New York Toronto London Auckland Sydney

It was Apple-Picking Day!

Mrs. Dee and the children had just arrived by bus at the Chester Apple Orchard. The owner greeted them.

"Hi," she said. "My name is Margie. I know you're all excited about picking apples today, but I'd like to show you something first. Come with me."

As the children followed Margie, Mrs. Dee reminded them to stay with their partners.

I can't wait to pick an apple, Albert thought as he walked beside Brendan.

Then, Albert sang this song:

It's Apple-Picking Day!
It's Apple-Picking Day!
I'll pick an apple from a tree,
And eat it right away.

The children went inside a large building.

"This is our store," Margie said. "It's where we sell all the things that we grow here."

"This pumpkin doesn't scare *me*," Brendan said.

"Now, let's go over to the apple orchard," Margie said as she led them outside. "Everyone will have a chance to pick one apple."

They walked until they reached a field with apple trees.

"Please, don't run," Margie said. "There are some slippery, mushy apples on the ground."

Margie gathered everyone next to one of the trees. Albert was surprised at how low the branches were.

"Wow!" Albert said. "I can reach out and touch the apples all by myself."

Mrs. Dee smiled at Albert.

"Please listen," said Margie. "There is a special way to take an apple off the tree. Instead of pulling on it, you just need to twist and turn. That way you won't hurt the tree. Look at how I'm doing it."

The children watched Margie turn an apple around and around until it fell off in her hand. Then she dipped the apple into a pail of water, dried it off, and took a big bite.

"Okay, now it's your turn," Margie said.
The children looked for apples to pick.
"Remember, you must stay where I can see you," Mrs. Dee said.
"That's a very important safety rule."

Tracy found a bright red apple. Just like Margie, she twisted it off, cleaned it, and took a great big bite.

"My apple is yummy!" Tracy said.

"Mine has lots of juice," said Danielle.

Albert searched for the reddest and roundest apple. He looked and looked until. . .

"I found it!" Albert yelled. "This is the best apple in the whole world."

Albert slowly twisted his apple. Finally, it came off the tree.

"Wow!" Albert said as he held up his apple. "I did it!"

Then Albert noticed something moving on his apple. He looked closer. It was a little worm!

"Ugh!" Albert said. "I can't eat an apple with a yucky worm in it." Albert looked sadly at his apple. "I don't want to eat this one," he said, "so I guess I'll put it on the ground."

Albert looked down and saw crushed apples everywhere.

"If I put the apple on the ground," he said, "someone might step on it and crush the worm. Even if he spoiled my apple, I still don't want him to get hurt."

Then, Albert noticed a spot with tall grass.

There's a safe place, he thought. *Nobody will step on the worm over there.*

Forgetting what Mrs. Dee said about staying together, Albert walked away from the group.

Meanwhile, the other children finished eating their apples and began playing in the field.

Brendan picked up two apples from the ground and held them over his eyes.

"Look at me!" he shouted. "I'm a big-eyed monster."

"It's time for lunch!" Mrs. Dee called. "Please come here."

All the children gathered around Mrs. Dee. All except Albert.

"Where's Albert?" Mrs. Dee said in a worried voice.

None of the children had seen him.

All at once, Albert popped out of the tall grass.

"Here I am," said Albert. "I was just . . ."

But before he could finish his explanation, Mrs. Dee interrupted him.

"Albert!" Mrs. Dee said in a strong voice. "I'm upset. I told you that we all need to stay together. Let's have a talk right now."

Margie started handing out the lunch bags as Mrs. Dee took Albert aside.

"Now, Albert," Mrs. Dee said. "What happened? Why did you walk into the tall grass where I couldn't see you?"

Albert told Mrs. Dee about the worm in his apple and how he didn't want it to get hurt.

"That was a sweet thing to do," Mrs. Dee said. "But you must come to me when you have a problem. It's not safe to walk away like that. Do you understand?"

"Yes," Albert said as he looked down.

Then, he began to cry.

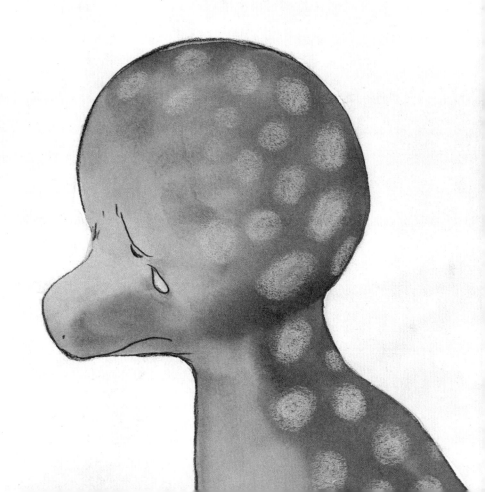

"What's the matter?" Mrs. Dee asked.

"Now you don't like me anymore," Albert said, wiping his eyes.

"Of course I like you," said Mrs. Dee. "Just because I was upset doesn't mean I stopped liking you."

Albert looked up at Mrs. Dee and smiled.

Then, he sang a new song:

A worm was in my apple,
Picked from the apple tree.
I should have brought it to my friend,
My teacher, Mrs. Dee.

Albert picked a new apple. And it was delicious!